TATA, the Tataviam Towhee

a Tribal Story

TATA, the Tataviam Towhee

a Tribal Story by

Alan Salazar
"Puchuk Ya'ia'c"

FERNANDEÑO TATAVIAM STORYTELLER

with Illustrations by

Mona Lewis

Sunsprite Publications

This project has been made possible in part by a generous grant
from the Fernandiño Tataviam Band of Mission Indians.

We would like to acknowledge the many people who helped bring this story to life.
Jazmin Aminian whose encouragement and support in every detail made all the difference.
We couldn't have done it without you. Merrily Eckel for that first fearless look at the work.
Kerry Meyers for your generosity and care to detail. Ash Good for your artistry in laying
out every aspect of the book to its best effect. We gratefully acknowledge Kimea Fatehi and
Rudy Ortega with the Tataviam tribe for their support and vast knowledge of tribal history.

Published by Sunsprite Publications
Ventura, California

Design and typesetting by Ash Good

ISBN: 978-1-7358195-0-1
LCCN:

FOR MY POP *who would say,*
"Did I ever tell you the story about
going deer hunting with Joe Barron?"
And I would say,
"Yes, Pop, you have told me a dozen times."
Then he would proceed to tell me the story.
I enjoyed it the thirteenth time
as much as I enjoyed it the first time.
AND TO THE NEXT GENERATION OF STORYTELLERS.

—AS

—————————

FOR MY DAUGHTERS. *who are my inspiration.*
AND FOR THE CHILDREN. *who still hear the stories*
of the land, and hold all its inhabitants
with tender hands and tender hearts.

—ML

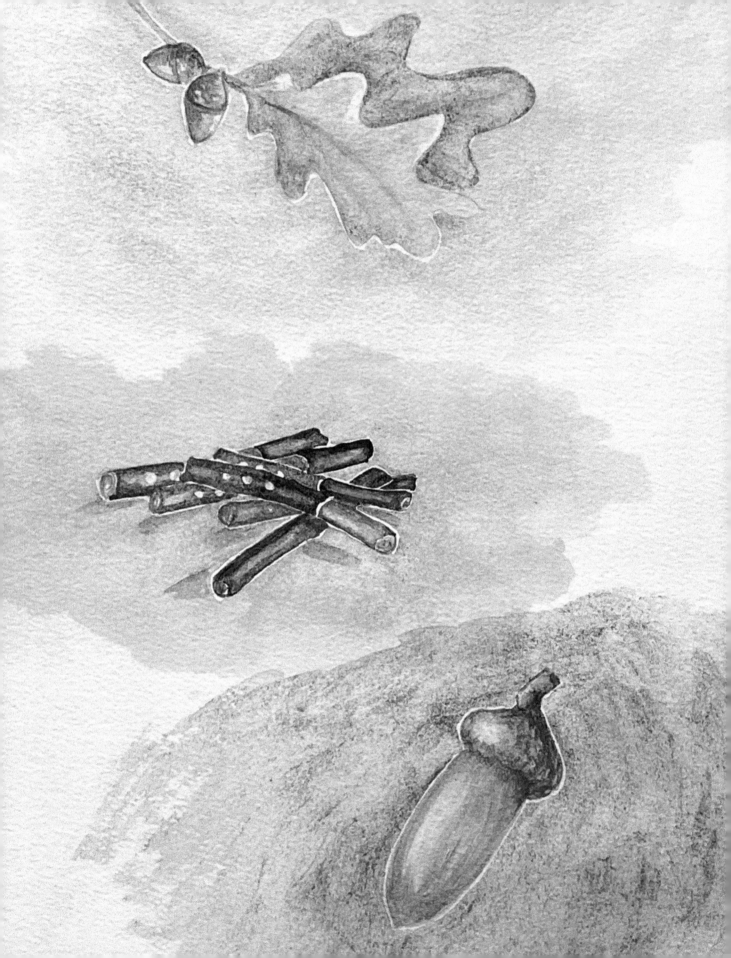

Contents

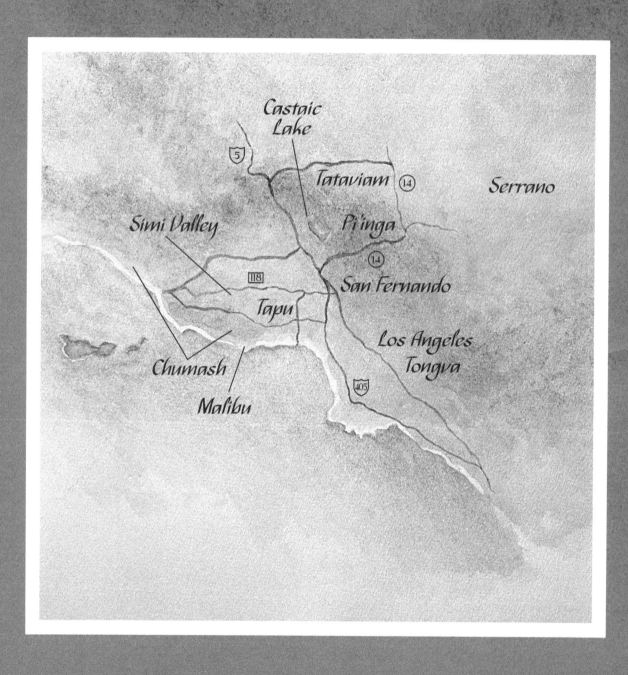

TATA, the Tataviam Towhee

This is a story of a young Tataviam Towhee bird. Today we call them California towhees, but Tata was hatched long ago near the Tataviam village of Pi'inga near modern day Castaic Lake, in southern California, hence Tataviam Towhee (pronounced tō -. hē).
The Towhee are small birds that hop and run from chaparral bush to chaparral bush looking for seeds and bugs to eat. They will occasionally fly, but never very high or very far.

Once there was a young Tataviam Towhee bird. His name was Tata. When Tata was young, his parents taught him how to hop and run from chaparral bush to chaparral bush, and where to find the best seeds and the juiciest bugs. Tata's parents also taught him how to fly.

They told him over and over, "Tata, never fly too high above the chaparral. And, never ever fly above the trees!!"

"Why?" asked Tata.

Tata's pop said, "There are giant killer birds — hawks, falcons, and eagles — that will eat you! They are fast, strong, and have sharp, sharp talons!!!"

Now, Tata was already five weeks old and like most teenagers he thought his parents were just trying to scare him. His parents seemed to be telling the truth, but like most teenagers he wanted to see these giant killer birds with his own eyes.

He landed on the top of the coyote brush and looked to his left, then to his right for those giant killer hawks, falcons, and eagles. He saw nothing.

He flew to the top of an elderberry tree.
He looked to his left, then to his right for
those killer hawks, falcons and eagles.
He saw nothing.

Then he flew to the top of the grandfather oak tree, a very large oak tree. He looked to his left, he looked to his right, and he did not see any giant killer hawks, falcons, or eagles.

Just then, Tata's friend, Juan the sparrow,
landed on the branch next to Tata.

Juan asked, "What are you doing way
up here my friend?"

Tata explained about the giant killer
birds his parents had warned him about
that he wanted to see for himself.

Tata said, "I looked all around, but I did
not see any giant killer birds."

At that moment, Juan said, "Look up,
my friend."

And Tata the Tataviam Towhee did.
And he saw a giant red-tailed hawk
circling high above him.

Then the hawk tucked his wings and
dived down towards the two small birds.
The two friends hopped into the center
of the oak tree for protection.

But... the red-tailed hawk was not after the two small birds. He was diving for a rattlesnake on the ground. He grabbed the rattlesnake in his powerful talons and flew off.

Tata was scared. He said to his friend, "That giant killer hawk just caught a rattlesnake — A RATTLESNAKE!!! Holy moly! My parents were telling me the truth!"

Juan said, " My parents told me the same thing. Maybe we should listen to them more closely?"

The two friends looked at each other for a moment, then both laughed and laughed.

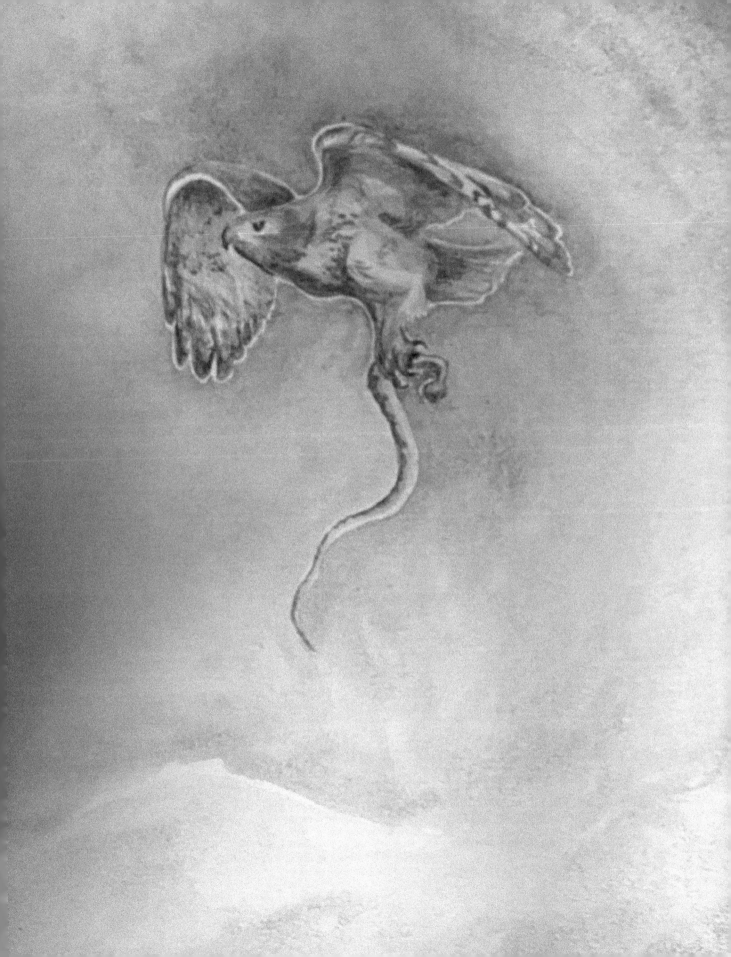

But after seeing that giant killer red-tailed hawk, the young birds did listen more closely to their parents. They just continued acting like they did not believe them. Yes, even teenage Tataviam Towhees can roll their eyes.

the end

About the Tataviam

by Alan Salazar "Puchuk Ya'ia'c"

Tataviam Territory in Southern California

The Tataviam are an indigenous tribe from northern Los Angeles county. The word Tataviam translates to "People Facing the Sun." We speak a Takic dialect from the Uto-Aztecan languages. Our territory covers the San Fernando Valley, Santa Clarita Valley, east to Lancaster and north into the mountains to Gorman. Today, the Tataviam villages are part of the coalition of lineages enrolled with the Fernandeño Tataviam Band of Mission Indians. While data suggests that we have been here for over 3000 years, our stories tell us that we have been here since time immemorial.

The Tataviam are hunters, gatherers and business people—yes, business people! We hunted and fished for many of the native animals: rabbits, deer, trout, squirrels, ducks, and geese, to name a few. We gathered acorns, yucca roots, brodiea roots, miner's lettuce, and wild berries. Most importantly, the Tataviam had business relationships with all of their neighboring villages. We traded the resources we had in abundance with the surrounding Yokut, Amutskajam (Kitanemuk), Simivitam (Chumash), Kaivitam (Serrano), and Komivitam (Tongva) lineages for thousands of years. For example, we traded deer hides for abalone shells from our Chumash neighbors. Then we traded those abalone shells to the Yokut peoples in the southern San Joaquin Valley, near modern day Bakersfield, for the right to hunt the tule Elk. We were surrounded by tribes that had valuable resources, and we traveled 50, 70, 100 miles or more to trade with them. We were hunters, gatherers and business people. We still are today. We run many businesses and we do our hunting and gathering at Vons and Trader Joe's (lol!).

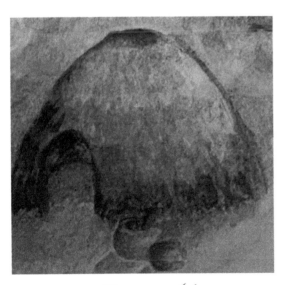

a Tataviam ki'j

Our villages were usually small, averaging 50 to 100 people in a village. Many of our villages were built along the south facing slopes of the mountains. That is why we were named, "People Facing the Sun."

Our houses were dome-shaped and our word for house is ki'j. Ki'j is pronounced "keech." Willow poles were dug into the ground in a 20 to 40 foot circle then tied together with dogbane twine. Dogbane is a native plant that many tribes in California used to make a very strong cordage. The willow frame was then covered with bulrush tule. Bulrush tule is a native plant that grows in ponds and along streams. It is light weight with a pithy center. It keeps your house warm in the winter and cool in the summer. It is an excellent insulation.

Most houses had work areas next to the ki'j. Rectangular shaped wood frames were used for drying animal hides. A work area with stone bowls and pestles for preparing acorn meal was also necessary.

Every village had a sweat lodge, usually near the river, stream or fresh water source. After going in the sweat lodge, our tribal members would rinse off in the river or stream to cleanse themselves. Being clean was important to us. Men, women and children all used the sweat lodge. Usually, the men and boys would sweat together, as would the women and girls.

Every village had a community ceremonial circle. The circle would be formed with rocks. It would have a simple shade structure made with willow poles and covered with bulrush tule. The circle would be used for various ceremonies. It was also used for storytelling, singing songs, dancing and playing games.

Every village had a group of religious leaders called Pahavitam (pa-ha'veet-tom) and a single spiritual leader called Pahavit. The Pahavitam was responsible for all ceremonies, like the winter solstice ceremony. The winter solstice ceremony was done on the shortest day of the year, December 21. They made offerings of tobacco to make sure the sun did not continue to get lower on the horizon. Naming ceremonies for newborn babies and ceremonies to pay respect to the animals we hunted were also common ceremonies.

Walnut Dice

Games were a large part of our daily life. We played games of chance, like the walnut dice game on page 33.

We played games of skill. Shinney, which is like field hockey, was played on large playing fields. The playing fields would be three to four times larger than our football fields. That is because there might be 20 to 40 players on each team, village against village. Hoop and pole is a game in which you throw a spear through a small hoop. Players would be 50 to 100 yards away from the six-inch in diameter hoop, so it took lots of skill. Foot races were also a large part of the games of skill we played.

We traveled everywhere by foot. So, knowing who was the fastest runner or who was the best long-distance runner was very important. Our best long-distance runners were also our messengers.

Messengers needed to have many skills besides being great runners. If we sent a messenger to a neighboring tribe to find out if they had an abundance of acorns, they had to negotiate. They might even have to speak a different language. The Chumash spoke a different language. The Kitanemuk, who live in the mountains north of us, spoke a different dialect of the same language. So, bartering skills, speaking several languages and being a great long-distance runner were all necessary to be a messenger.

home
ki'j

hello
hamiinat

rattlesnake
huung't

red-tailed hawk
kwaa'c

elderberry tree
kwur

oak tree
syutka

Tataviam Words

Starting in 1797, the Tataviam were forcibly brought to the San Fernando Mission. The mission priests believed we were inferior, subhuman, or savages. We were treated very poorly. Our families were separated. The men were placed in one structure; women in another structure; and, children in yet another structure. We were forced to work from sunrise to sunset, and fed very little food. We were never paid for our work. We were slaves. We were not allowed to speak our language and would be beaten if we did. If we tried to escape back to our villages, the soldiers from the mission would forcibly bring us back. Due to the long hard work days and being fed very little food, we became weak. In our weakened condition many of the Tataviam people died from diseases. After several years of the mission period, things got even worse for the Tataviam people.

By the 1820s, our ancestors had to endure the Mexican regime. Our Tataviam people negotiated with the Mexican governors for land. This is how we gained land rights to several land grants, including Rancho Encino (which was held by my great-great-grandmother), Rancho Cahuenga, Rancho Tujunga, Rancho Escorpion, and more. These grants were supposed to be protected in the American period, but our lands were too valuable among a booming population of settlers who needed access to our natural water sources. Within the first few years of the American regime, when California became a state in 1850, our ancestors were dispossessed of all our lands. Only one land grant remained in my tribe's possession in present-day San Fernando, California, but was eventually removed from us after a costly and devastating ten-year legal battle against an ex-California senator.

When California became a state in 1850, thousands more tribal people throughout the state died. A brutal state policy to get rid of all California Indians was put into place by the first governor of California. By 1880, most of the Tataviam were gone.

The few Tataviam that survived this extremely difficult time fought to save their tribal ways. Today, there are more than 1000 Tataviam tribal members. We are bringing back our language and many of our tribal ways. We are getting back some of our traditional land. Today, we continue to hunt, gather and trade with the Chumash people, Tongva people, Serrano people, Yokut people and Kitanemuk people as we have for thousands of years.

This is just a brief history of my Tribe. I hope you enjoyed reading it and a learned a little about my Tataviam tribe from California.

For more history information, please visit www.tataviam-nsn.us

For more information about Alan Salazar's educational programs and story telling please visit www.mynativestories.com

— Alan Salazar
"Puchuk Ya'ia'c" (Fast Runner)
Tribal Elder

playing the
walnut
dice game

There are 6 Walnut halves to be used for the dice.

The shells may be inlaid with tar and abalone or used plain.

Any number of players may play.

Each player starts with 6 sticks for keeping score.

Sticks were traditionally willow sticks, 4" long, peeled and decorated. But, any stick would work. Popsicle sticks are easy to paint and make good counting sticks.

Players take turns throwing the dice.

Points are awarded like this:

6 flat sides up—2 points

6 round sides up—2 points

3 up and 3 down—1 point

Any combination of 2 and 4 or 1 and 5—0 points

When someone throws the dice and wins points, all the other players give the winner the corresponding number of sticks.

For example, if all the flat sides land down, each person gives the one who threw the dice 2 of their sticks.

A player continues to throw the dice until they don't win any points, then the dice go to the next player in turn.

The game continues until one person has all the sticks.

Three hundred years ago, lots of people played at once. If 8 or 10 people played, the game could go on for hours. It might even go all night long!

If you don't want to play with sticks, simply decide how long your game will go and keep score another way.

For example, the person who has the most points after 20 minutes wins the game.

Have fun!

About the
Illustrations

by Mona Lewis

Paint Stones found in the Tataviam territory

All the illustrations

in this book were made with stones and soil respectfully foraged from within the Tataviam territory.

I found some of these paint stones near my home in Chatsworth, which sits on the border of Tataviam territory. Some stones came from the missions where Tataviam people were enslaved, and hold a little of that hard story within them. One of the black paints was created from charcoal left in the wake of a brush fire which destroyed large swaths of chaparral one very hot summer here. The other black was made by roasting indigenous cucumber seeds, using a traditional recipe.

*Palatte of colors found
in Tataviam territory*

I ground each color by hand to make the paint for these illustrations.

The only exception in the collection is the blue Vivianite ocher, which I used mostly for the sky tones. It comes from the north shore of Washington state and Vancouver. The Vivianite found there was formed thousands of years ago as the result of a tsunami which flooded the shoreline leaving phosphorous and iron to interact and oxidize into the blue ocher you see. It has been used traditionally for thousands of years by the Coast Salish and neighboring tribal people in the north for painting totem poles. Colors like this are not for sale, but I was able to trade for it and am honored it include it here.

— Mona Lewis, Illustrator

For more from artist Mona Lewis
visit www.sunspritehandwork.com.
follow @sunspritehandwork
on Instagram and Facebook or email
sunspritehandwork@yahoo.com

Try Making
Pigment
Yourself!

On your next walk around your neighborhood, slow your pace and look carefully in the soil where you live. See if you can find rocks that are soft and have some color. You can test to see if they are soft enough by rubbing them on the back of a tile, or any hard rock near by. If they easily leave a mark, they will be good for pigment.

Next, gently tap your pigment rock with a hammer until it is broken into small pieces. If you have a mortar and pestle, place the pieces in the mortar and grind to a fine powder.

If you don't have a mortar and pestle, grind the small rocks to a powder using circular motions with your hammer. Pour your powdered pigment through a small strainer to sift out the larger pieces. Now your powdered pigment is ready to use!

You may add a little water to this powder and paint with it, but it is easy to make a lovely picture just by rubbing the dry pigment directly on paper. Find instructions to draw your own towhee on page 40 and coloring pages on page 44.

Find soft, colored stones and
break them into pieces

Grind the stone pieces
into a fine powder

Store your pigment powders
in small containers

Rub dry pigment on paper or
mix with water for wet paint

How to Paint a
Towhee
Step-by-Step

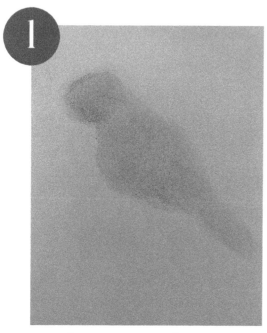

Take a little powder on your finger tip and rub it in a circular motion onto the paper to create the head and body

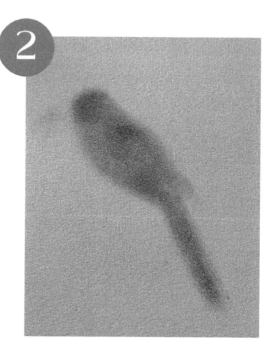

Add a darker tone for the face and tail feathers

You can create a towhee by rubbing your dry pigments directly on the paper. Follow the steps below! For a video tutorial on drawing a towhee, visit the Sunsprite channel at ▶ youtu.be/2K--OTDtL5I *Tips: Don't worry if you can't find exactly the same colors here. If you find one light stone, one dark, one cool colored stone and one warm, that's plenty to paint with! For step four, follow the charcoal making instructions on page 42. You can also use a pencil for the details, but it's fun to make your own charcoal if an adult can help you make a fire!*

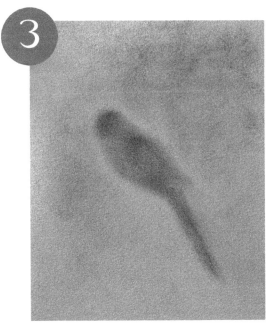

If you can find a grey rock or even some dark colored soil, use that to rub in a background color

Next, make some charcoal (or use a pencil) to draw in the details

How to Make
Charcoal
Step-by-Step

Gather some small sticks. Rose bush cuttings, willow sticks and grape vine cuttings work very well, but almost any little stick will do.

Find a small tin box with a lid. The box that mints come in is perfect, or a small cookie tin. Cut your sticks small enough to fit in the box. Put them in and close the lid.

You'll need an adult's help to make charcoal.

Follow the steps below. Tips: If no tin box is available, you could also wrap the sticks in aluminum foil and seal the edges well, making sure not much air gets in. If you use a larger tin, like a cookie tin, leave it in the fire for a longer than an hour.

Build a small bonfire, or one in the fireplace or a wood burning stove. Using tongs or another good tool, place the box of twigs in the center of the fire.

After about an hour, carefully remove the tin from the fire. Once it is cool, open it and draw with your charcoal!

Alan Salazar
"Puchuk Ya'ia'c"
(Fast Runner)

Alan Salazar is a traditional storyteller, a native educator, and a native monitor/consultant. He is a tribal elder in both the Fernandeño Tataviam and Ventureño Chumash tribes. He is a tribal spiritual advisor and a traditional paddler of Chumash canoes. His native ancestors were brought into the San Fernando Mission starting in 1799. Like many Fernandeño natives, his family has Tataviam ancestry from the Tataviam village of Chaguayanga near Castaic, California and Tochonanga in present-day Pico Canyon, California. His Chumash ancestry is from the Chumash village of Ta'apu near Simi Valley, California. He continues to actively protect his ancestor's village sites and tribal territories.

Alan has been actively involved with several native indigenous groups. He is a founding member of the Kern County Native American Heritage Preservation Council, Chumash Maritime Association, and a member of the California Indian Advisory Council for the Santa Barbara Museum of Natural History, a community advisor with the Ventura County Indian Education Consortium for over 25 years, and is currently active on the Elder's Council for the Fernandeño Tataviam Band of Mission Indians.

As a member of the Chumash Maritime Association, Alan helped build the first working traditional Chumash plank canoe (tomol) in modern times, and has paddled in plank canoes for over 22 years. The Chumash of antiquity used their tomols to travel extensively between the California coast and the Channel Islands. They had villages on each of the islands, and friends and families traveled inter-island to fish, visit and trade. Alan is one the most experienced Chumash paddlers in modern times, participating in every modern re-enactment of the crossings starting from Oxnard to Santa Cruz Island.

Alan has also been involved with teaching youths about native American cultures for over 25 years. He has created educational programs at schools, museums and cultural events both in the United States and in Great Britain.

As a spiritual adviser within the Fernandeño Tataviam and Chumash communities, Alan leads ceremonies and prayer circles during traditional native indigenous gatherings. He was raised to be proud of his native indigenous heritage and takes pride in being a positive role model and a respected elder.

This book is an original story that Alan wrote in the spirit of Tataviam storytelling. It is his sincere hope that you will enjoy it and learn something about this beautiful land.

Mona Lewis

Mona's family comes from the United Kingdom, France, and Scandinavia. She is a watercolor artist, dancer, and teacher of handwork in Waldorf education since 1996. She is co-director of the Waldorf Practical Arts Teacher Training program associated with the Southern California Waldorf Teacher Training Institute. Mona trains artists, teachers and home-schooling families in the plant-dye arts and in the practical arts of the Waldorf curriculum.

Using traditional historical dye plants such as indigo, madder, and weld, as well as local indigenous dye plants such as black walnut and costal sagebrush, she created a plant dye garden on the campus at Highland Hall Waldorf School. Students from Kindergarten through the 12th grade participate in caring for the garden from seed to harvest. Using these plants to dye fibers for their handwork projects, students learn about the cultures in which these dye plants originate through hands-on experience of these ancient cultural arts.

Mona has worked extensively behind the scenes at Highland Hall Waldorf School in the areas of cultural diversity, school governance and festival development. Working in association with local tribal elders, students at Highland Hall learn about the history of the tribal people on whose land the school is situated.

In 2020, celebrating Indigenous People's Day, Highland Hall created a plaque honoring the local indigenous tribes to be displayed on campus. This plaque features a statement of land acknowledgement, and a promise to the first peoples that they will "lift up their stories, culture and community." It was accompanied by the planting of two California Oak trees in a place of honor on the campus. Tribal elders came to offer blessings and stories as is now customary for this annual event. Also, for the first time, the tribal president (or chief), Rudy Ortega and his sons attended, bringing their traditional "Bird Songs" for the community. The event was televised via Zoom to the whole Highland Hall student body.

Through feather
　　and blade, on petal
and soft breezes,
　　these stories still flow
through the land,
　　inviting us to listen . . .
for now we are
　　a part of it too.

CPSIA information can be obtained
at www.ICGtesting.com
Printed in the USA
JSHW011301110222
22768JS00002B/28

9 781735 819501